MW00743651

Dedicated To: All the Nanas and Grampas of the world who
share their time, love and wisdom with their grandchildren.

Richard M. Wainwright
Ron Walotsky

I owe a great debt to thousands of people who have touched my life deeply: my wonderful parents, inspirational teachers and coaches, countless students, friends, and talented authors who provided me with hours of vicarious adventures, challenged my ideas and beliefs and made me stretch and expand my concepts and understanding of the world and life. All contributed to my efforts to write meaningful stories for people.

There is space to mention only so few: my beloved wife, D'Ann, who was truly "the wind beneath my wings", my talented illustrators and friends; Jack Crompton, Carolyn S. Dvorsack, Ron Walotsky, and Judith Partelow, superb narrator of my books. My love and thanks to lifelong friends the Woodwards, Coes, Sabantys, Lumsdens, Greenes, Cruickshanks, McGourtys, Nelsons, Brunets, Woodworths, Hanks, Svendsens, Kozackos, Thompsons, Harts, Dubins, Scotts, Berts, Burners, and so many dear people who live on Cape Cod, in Florida or are scattered across the U.S. and Canada. I will never forget the encouragement and support from people like Mary Higgins Clark, the Ulmans, Rita Horner, my mother Bee, father Edwin and my mother and father-in-law Nina and Charles, our boys Fredy, Cesar and Pablo, colleagues at Eagles Nest, Palm Coast and in Ecuador. These are but a handful of people whose love and friendship enriched our lives. I want to mention Dr. Heber "Grampa" Kimbal, Keewaydinese, the Brynildsens, the Rogers, fellow crafters and all whose love and comfort sustained me through the darkest days of my life. And Judy, who has made it possible to once again experience the joy of loving and sharing the blessings of life. *Richard*

FAMILY LIFE
PUBLISHING

Published by Family Life Publishing,
Box 2010, Dennis, MA 02638, and Box 353844, Palm Coast, FL 32135

Text Copyright c 1997 Richard M. Wainwright   Illustrations Copyright c 1997 Ron Walotsky

All rights reserved

First Edition

Printed in Singapore by Tien Wah Press. Published in the United States of America

Library of Congress Cataloging in Publication Data
Wainwright, Richard M., Nana, Grampa and Tecumseh / written by Richard M.Wainwright:
illustrated by Ron Walotsky.– 1st ed.
p. cm.
Summary: The time that a brother and sister spend with their grandfather, particularly with his special tree in the forest near the family farm, help them deal with their own father's death, their mother's remarriage, and Grampa's own passing.
ISBN# 0-9619566-7-4
[1. Grandfathers--Fiction. 2. Brothers and sisters--Fiction 3. Death--Fiction]
I. Walotsky, Ron, ill. II. Title
PZ7. W13117Nan 1997
[Fic] -- DC21   97-5
CIP
AC

Nana, Grampa & Tecumseh

Written by Richard M. Wainwright
Illustrated by Ron Walotsky

TO_____

Try to make each day in your life
A DAY TO REMEMBER.

Best Wishes,
Richard M. Wainwright   Ron Walotsky

FROM_____

Chapter 1

Grampa opened the front door, looking as tall as one of the pine trees that surrounded his home. A grizzly bear of a man, his gray beard gently gave way to a tanned face creased from years of working hard and a smile that seemed to stretch from ear to ear. Grampa was big and strong and in one easy motion swept the twins into his arms as their mom laughed. They lassoed him around his neck and at the same time kissed him on his cheeks. They loved their grandparents very much. "How are my favorite twins?" Grampa roared, "and of course, Gail, my wonderful daughter-in-law? We're glad to see you. Amanda, Jonathan—your rooms are all ready for you, right, Nana?"

Their grandmother smiled and nodded. After more hugs and kisses the twins left their suitcases at the bottom of the stairs and followed their noses into the kitchen. They could smell the heavenly aroma of warm chocolate chip cookies. Today was Friday. Several hours earlier Mom had picked up the twins at school. Her new job selling real estate required her to work Saturdays and Sundays and their grandparents suggested Amanda and Jonathan spend weekends, when possible, with them. The twins didn't have a father. Their dad had died in a car accident two years before and they missed him more than they could talk about. They didn't think life was fair.

"Jonathan, what are you and Amanda studying in junior high school now?" Nana asked as the twins hungrily devoured the delicious cookies.

Jonathan was thinking, *Nobody can make cookies like grandmas. They are definitely the best.* "What did you say, Nana?" Jonathan asked.

"Jonathan was day-dreaming again, Nana," Amanda said. "There's a very pretty girl who sits next to him in most classes. I wouldn't be surprised if Jonathan was back in school whispering with Ashley."

"Be serious, Sis," Jonathan replied with a big grin, "you know the only girls in my life are you, Mom and Nana. Please pass the plate of cookies. Tell Nana the straight scoop so I can continue eating."

Amanda raised her eyebrows, smiled and continued, "Right now we are working on algebra, geography, history, Spanish, natural science and of course, lots of reading and writing. By the end of the year we must publish a small book with dedications, covers and everything. Jonathan and I plan to work on the book together, but we still haven't decided what to write about. Maybe you and Grampa can give us some ideas."

Grampa spoke up, "Well, tomorrow, if it's a good day, I'll take you to meet an old friend of mine and your father's. His name is Tecumseh. Maybe he will share some thoughts with you, and if you listen closely, give you some ideas for your book."

"Who is Tecumseh?" the twins asked in unison but Grampa only winked and told them to wait until tomorrow. Mom got up from the table and prepared to leave, as it was a two-hour drive back home. She told the twins to be good, take care of Nana and Grampa and then kissed all good night. She would be back Sunday evening.

The next morning, Jonathan raised the shade of his window to let in a warm and brilliant sun. It was going to be a beautiful day.

"Breakfast in 15 minutes," Nana called, "and don't forget to wash your face and brush those teeth." By the time Jonathan was ready to go downstairs to the kitchen, the wonderful aroma of pancakes, bacon and hot chocolate had reached him. Amanda, always the early riser, was helping Nana make the pancakes, so Grampa and Jonathan set the table.

"Eat up, gang." Grampa advised. "We have some hiking to do before seeing Tecumseh. Nana, maybe a few sandwiches for my knapsack would be a good idea."

After finishing breakfast, doing the dishes and making their beds the twins put on their coats and, with Grampa in the lead, started across a field toward the trees. Grampa's old house had been built over 100 years ago. The government had given his family special permission to remain inside the borders of what was now part of a huge national forest. His father, grandfather and great-grandfather had lived in the old homestead for three generations. Their families had grown up on the edge of wilderness: hunting in the forest, clearing land near the house for gardens and building barns for cows and horses. Grampa and Nana still raised a few chickens for eggs and had a small garden for fresh vegetables, but the barns were now empty.

As they entered the forest, it became darker and cooler. The sun's rays were partly blocked by the tall pine trees. They walked silently on the soft carpet of pine needles. "Everything smells so fresh and clean, Grampa," Amanda observed. "Do you know the name of that little bird with a black cap that seems to be following us, skipping from branch to branch?"

"That's one of the friendliest and probably bravest little birds in the forest," Grampa replied. "It's a chickadee. He knows I have a treat for him. But he is not the only bird you will see. Tecumseh and I have many feathered and animal friends. I am sure you will see several more today."

The forest warmed from the spring sun. Grampa stopped and pointed out young plants that were beginning to push through the pine needles. The twins learned how Bearberry got its name, and that young fiddlehead ferns were good to eat. Amanda held her nose as they passed the skunk cabbage that grew in marshy spots near a brook. Carefully, they examined beautiful lady slippers. Grampa spotted a patch of wild lily of the valley and all knelt down to smell the lovely scent.

Over the years, Grampa and Nana had worn a path through the forest as they had taken this route hundreds of times. In fact, Grampa called it *Nana's Walk*. The trail zigzagged until it came to a rocky ledge that looked over a beautiful green meadow. "A good many years ago lightning started a fire in this part of the forest," Grampa explained. "It burned this area badly before a torrential rain put the fire out. Every living plant, from wild flowers to the tallest tree, died. In time, the wind, rain and snow forced the dead trees to fall. Slowly they decomposed and became food for new plants and young trees. You can still see a few silver-colored branches from the old trees above the ground, indicating where a big tree fell."

On the other side of the meadow pine trees covered the side of a hill. " Listen, can you hear something different?" asked Grampa. They stopped walking and stood still. "Birds," Jonathan replied.

Amanda guessed, "Is that a squirrel chattering nearby?"

" Yes and no," Grampa said, "I hear those sounds too, but can you hear the laughing stones?" Amanda and Jonathan shook their heads and looked at each other, wondering if Grampa was teasing them. Laughing stones?

"You'll hear them better in a few minutes," Grampa said. The three began to climb through the pines. At the top of the hill there were fewer trees. Below them the land gently sloped toward a wide, shimmering river with lots of boulders. The tops of the boulders stuck up here and there and the splashing of the water on and around the rocks made funny, gurgling sounds—Grampa's laughing stones.

The twins' gaze traveled down the gentle, green slope to a gigantic tree. A short distance behind the tree the sun's diamonds danced on the surface of the rushing blue waters. Crossing the river with their eyes, they slowly climbed above the tops of the never-ending forest to the snow-capped mountains that appeared to touch the fluffy clouds tumbling across the sky.

Grampa led the way toward the river. Near the edge a lone oak tree majestically towered well over one hundred feet skyward. The huge tree had a trunk diameter of close to four feet. Some of its big roots were only partly buried and spread in all directions great distances from the trunk of the tree. Grampa stepped on the thick carpet of soft green moss that surrounded the gigantic tree. Grampa looked up and began to speak. "Greetings, Tecumseh, I have brought my grandchildren Jonathan and Amanda to meet you today. Please share your wisdom with them, as you have with me and my family these many years." Grampa was talking to a tree? Grampa spoke to the twins. "Tecumseh has lived a long, long time and knows more than I could ever learn. We have shared many days together here. The plants, animals, birds, and this beautiful river have been my teachers. This river's water remains pure and clear. Sadly, there are not many rivers left in the world like this one. The Indians who lived near this beautiful river and fished and hunted along its banks called it 'Manitou's River'—the river of the Great Spirit."

"How did Tecumseh get his name?" Amanda asked, chuckling. "I didn't hear him speak." The twins still weren't sure if Grampa was serious or fooling.

"Well, you and Jonathan find a soft spot under Tecumseh's branches and I will sit down beside you and tell you how this magnificent scarlet oak got its name.

"When I was your age I often came to this spot with my Grampa—Grampa Daniel. He loved this glen, loved life and loved every living thing that is part of our world. He even had a good word for those pesky ants that somehow knew just when we were about to eat our lunch. Grampa Daniel used to say, 'Never you mind, we always got enough to share so give 'em their due.' Guess he was right, 'cause I can't recall ever heading home hungry with Grampa Daniel.

"Long before Grampa Daniel, there was Grampa Caleb. He too sat right here under the branches of this old oak tree. Grampa Caleb was your great-great-great-great-grandfather. He came from Europe. His son was Grampa Thomas. Grampa Caleb taught Thomas all he knew 'bout everything' and his sons have passed on his stories and knowledge down to each generation of our family.

"In Grampa Caleb's time many Indians lived in these parts. He and his family came to know many of these Native Americans well and learned much from them.

"One day, when Caleb was a boy and fishing right here, a tall, dark Indian appeared out of nowhere. Caleb jumped up, startled and afraid, but the Indian's big smile and hand raised in peace calmed him. The Indian rubbed his stomach and pointed at Caleb, who didn't understand. Then he made a fist and placed it on his chest and said, 'Tecumseh' and again pointed at Caleb. Grampa Caleb thought he understood and placed his hand on his chest and said, 'Caleb.'

"The Indian slowly repeated his name, 'C A L E B,' and smiled. Then he raised an open hand before turning toward the river. He fitted an arrow to his bow and silently entered the water, making no more noise than a shadow. Everything the Indian did seemed to be in slow motion, but in less than the blink of an eye Tecumseh's bow was raised and the arrow flew. Quickly he retrieved the whirling arrow, which held fast a large, thrashing trout. Tecumseh returned to shore smiling and then did a strange thing. Strange then to Grampa Caleb. Tecumseh held the fish high toward the sun and spoke in his language for almost a minute.

"Years later, Grampa Caleb learned that Tecumseh had thanked the fish's spirit for giving up its life so Tecumseh and the boy could eat. He had also thanked the spirit of the sun for not casting his shadow near the fish, which would have scared it away. After speaking, Tecumseh took out a sharp knife, cleaned the fish and then gathered a few rocks near the shore to make a small ring. It wasn't long before a fire was crackling under and around the fish, which rested on a flat rock slightly above the flames. With one hand, he drew a picture of a leaf and pointed to Caleb. Grampa Caleb understood and ran to find some large green leaves. Lunch was ready when he returned. Tecumseh smiled and placed the cooked fish on the leaves. He broke off a piece and gave it to Caleb. They ate in silence, but Caleb grinned a lot and rubbed his tummy. When they had finished, he and Tecumseh put out the fire and shook hands. Without a word, the Indian turned and quickly disappeared into the forest.

"Grampa Caleb never saw Tecumseh again, but he named this great oak tree 'Tecumseh' in honor of that man. He spent the rest of his life learning all he could about this land and the first Americans who lived here. This was his favorite spot in the world, and here he shared his life's stories with his son and grandson. Years later, Grampa Daniel told me that story. This glen has become my favorite spot, too."

Grampa reached into his pocket and took out a small leather pouch. He untied the drawstring and shook out a shining white pointed stone. "This is a beautifully made quartzite arrow point. It is over one hundred years old. Grampa Daniel found two near the river on our last visit. He had searched along the bank for years for an arrow point of this quality, but had never found one. That day he told me to sit here beside Tecumseh. Almost like someone was guiding him, he went down to the river, walked past several large rocks, and stopped in front of two gray stones. He knelt down and found one quartzite arrow point under each. He gave me one. Grampa Daniel believed it was Tecumseh's spirit that guided him that day. Who knows? I have looked for years but have never found another finely crafted quartzite arrowhead.

"Indians carried amulets and medicine bags. Amulets were objects worn around the neck as charms against evil or injury. They believed these pieces would protect them and bring them good luck during their lives. When they died, those things were buried with them. This white arrow point has been my talisman or good luck piece. Maybe the spirit that guided Grampa Daniel will help you find an arrow point someday." Grampa winked, and said, "No matter what you believe, it's always fun to hunt for Indian artifacts. We can learn much from the Native Americans who first loved this land."

Amanda and Jonathan looked closely at the shiny arrowhead. Grampa began unpacking his knapsack and spreading a small tablecloth on the ground. Out came Nana's sandwiches, fruit punch, apples, bananas and a bag of homemade cookies. Grampa raised his eyebrows and spoke, "I think Nana thought we were going to stay away for a week." Grampa chuckled as Jonathan handed the arrowhead back to his grandfather.

    As they began to eat lunch, Jonathan asked how Indians made their arrowheads. No other question could have pleased Grampa more. Like his grandfathers and father, Grampa had read all the books he could find on the history and ways of American Indians. "Well, first an Indian needed to find stone we call flint," Grampa said softly. "Talented Indians who were able to make fine arrow points were called flintknappers. The flintknapper would place a piece of leather on his thigh and then with a hammer stone begin to flake off pieces, roughly shaping the flint. When it was close to the shape he wanted the flintknapper took a sharpened deer horn to backflake from the sides. Quartzite is very difficult to flake, so this final stage took time, patience and skill, as a wrong move could ruin the arrow point. Do you think you have the idea?"

    The twins smiled and nodded. Grampa put his arrow point back in his pouch and then put a finger to his lips. Slowly he turned his head to the right and smiled. Hopping into view were two cottontail rabbits. Then he pointed above his head, and Amanda and Jonathan looked up to see that a squirrel and several birds were spectators to their lunch. Lowering their eyes, just a few feet away the head of a little chipmunk popped up above one of Tecumseh's exposed roots.

"Our friends will help finish any leftovers," Grampa whispered as he reached into his pocket for some sunflower seeds. He held his hand out straight and a few moments later a chickadee gently landed on his fingertips and studied the selection before taking a seed in his beak and flying back to a branch to crack open his lunch. The twins sat mesmerized as Grampa's chickadee flew back and forth. Then Grampa put seeds in Amanda's hand. It wasn't long before the chickadee flew down. Soon it was Jonathan's turn, and the chickadee continued to fly back and forth. Amazed, the twins then watched Grampa coax the the squirrel and chipmunk closer as he placed pieces of bread and a cookie just beyond the tablecloth.

"Remember, these are wild animals. Chipmunks, squirrels and raccoons can bite and may carry diseases, so never try to feed them by hand." After lunch, Grampa said he would pack up while the twins walked along the shore.

"Old man sun is definitely heading home," Grampa said. "It's time for us to do the same." Amanda and Jonathan had been turning over rocks, looking for arrowheads. They startled a few frogs, watched water bugs doing their crazy dance, and annoyed a couple of crayfish, which didn't like being disturbed, but they didn't find any Indian artifacts.

"Can we go fishing the next time we visit Tecumseh, Grampa?" Jonathan asked.

"We sure can," Grampa replied. "There's a nice deep hole just around the bend, and if we're lucky maybe we will cook our lunch just like Tecumseh did for Grampa Caleb."

Chapter II

The next several months went by fast for the twins. They were busy with school work and sports on weekends, but there was always time to telephone Nana and Grampa. Their mother met a man she seemed to like very much, and introduced Mr. Dubin to the twins. He seemed nice and took them to the zoo, the science museum and a professional baseball game. Amanda and Jonathan liked him, but of course no one would ever take the place of their father.

"Hi, Grampa!" Amanda began on the phone. "How are you and Nana doing? Classes are over—summer vacation, here we come. Tonight, Jonathan and I are packing our suitcases. Do you think you can stand us for a few weeks?"

"We're ready and anxious to see you both," Grampa replied. It has been too long. We have missed you and want to hear all about how your school year ended. I understand you and Jonathan got very good grades, and that makes Nana and I very happy. Nana is making some chocolate chip cookies right now, so you can tell Jonathan the cookie jar will be full by the time you arrive tomorrow."

The next night, the twins were settled in at their grandparent's home. They told Nana and Grampa everything that had happened during the past months, and of course Nana and Grampa were delighted to see some of the twins' papers and report cards. Jonathan had pictures of his baseball team, and Amanda had ones of her softball team, along with snapshots of their trips with Mr. Dubin. It had been a long day. Soon the twins were yawning, and Nana hustled them off to bed. As they climbed the stairs, Jonathan reminded Grampa of his promise to take them fishing.

"Don't worry—everything is ready." Grampa winked. "I even told Tecumseh you were coming. First thing tomorrow we begin by digging for worms." Amanda wrinkled her nose—Jonathan grinned. "Now, off to bed both of you—pleasant dreams." After a hug and kiss the twins climbed the stairs to bed.

The next morning, much to Jonathan's surprise and mild disappointment, Amanda showed no fear of snatching up the wiggly night crawlers as Grampa turned the earth at the side of the vegetable garden. There would be no teasing his sister today. "Gotcha," she shouted as another large worm tried to hide under a clump of dirt.

"The tin can is filling up fast, Grampa," Amanda observed. "I hope the fish appreciate all our work this morning."

"Thanks to your keen eyes, I think we have enough worms. Jonathan, put a little dirt in the can and let's go eat. I don't know about you two, but I'm hungry." The twins smiled—Grampa had a big appetite. After breakfast, Grampa suggested they all check the tent and sleeping bags, and pack the backpacks to make sure they had everything needed to spend several days with Tecumseh.

It didn't take long for the twins and Grampa to pack the supplies, extra clothes, sleeping bags and tent. Grampa carried the largest backpack, but the twins had hefty loads, too. They started out single file. Jonathan led, then Amanda and their whistling Grampa. The pace was slow and steady. Every half-hour they stopped to rest, have a snack or drink some water. It was warm and a little muggy. A few mosquitoes urged them on, and in two hours they were setting up the tent under Tecumseh's branches.

Jonathan couldn't wait to get fishing, but Grampa said there were jobs to do first, including building the fire circle near the river, lining it with stones, and making a latrine back in the woods. The twins also dug a shallow ditch around the tent in case it rained. The clothes and sleeping bags were placed in the tent and the food stored in a hanging bag from a nearby tree.

"Now," said Grampa, "anyone for fishing?"

Grampa rigged the rods. Putting a finger to his lips, he beckoned the twins to follow. Amanda carried the worms and Jonathan carried a fishing-tackle box. As silently as possible, they followed Grampa along the shore until they came to a bend where big boulders jutted out into the river. Mid-river, the water boiled, but in front of the boulders a deep, mirror-like pool sparkled in the late morning sun.

Moving a little way back from the boulders, Grampa showed the twins how to bait the hooks. Then he gave each a worm so they could bait their own hooks. It was squiggly business, but with Grampa's coaching it wasn't long before the twins were ready to fish. One at a time Grampa quietly led them to boulders in front of the beautiful pool. Then they cast the worms as far into the pool as possible and sat stone still. Grampa watched. Nothing happened!!!

At first the twins stared intently at their lines, but in a few minutes their eyes wandered to the rushing river, then to the trees and a lone red-tailed hawk that lazily circled high above them.

Wham! At practically the same instant, two rods were pulled down and lines shot out straight almost pulling the fishing poles from their hands. By the time Jonathan and Amanda yanked their rods, the lines were slack. Their hands shook, their hearts pounded, and they turned and looked at Grampa with sad faces. First he smiled, then Grampa broke into a big grin and laughed until tears came to his eyes.

Grampa finally stopped laughing but was still grinning as he told them. "Don't look so unhappy, you just learned your first lesson from teacher trout. He or she thanks you very much for lunch. Trout are pretty smart, and if you going to catch one, there's no wool-gathering on the job. Now come and get some more worms."

A few more worms became a fish's lunch before first Amanda and then Jonathan hooked a beautiful rainbow trout. Grampa showed each of them how to take it off the hook and string the shimmering silvery fish. Amanda and Jonathan were thrilled, and at the same time a little sad, as they looked at the beautiful fish. Then Grampa took one of the rods and in no time landed another trout.

"Now we have all the food we need," Grampa announced, "so any more fish you catch, we return."

Amanda and Jonathan looked at each other and smiled. They understood Grampa and remembered the story of Grampa Caleb and Tecumseh. Grampa substituted barbless hooks and the twins baited and cast their lines again.

Jonathan and Amanda eventually caught two more trout. Grampa showed them how to gently take the hook out of the fish's mouth and then return it to the river. Minutes turned into hours. Finally, Grampa said it was time to return to camp and prepare supper. The afternoon had flown. For Jonathan and Amanda, it seemed they had been fishing for just a few moments. Their stomachs began to growl, so they knew that wasn't true. Grampa carried the rods, Jonathan the tackle box, and Amanda three trout on a string.

Near the shore, Grampa got out a cutting board and showed the twins how to carefully use the sharp fishing knife to clean a trout, and then he let the twins try. He watched their every move as they cleaned the fish and took the trout to the river to wash them. Afterward, the twins washed carrots and onions, and then sliced them before wrapping them and a fish in aluminum foil. Grampa scrubbed the potatoes while Jonathan and Amanda gathered dead branches and kindling. It wasn't long before a pile of wood was stacked neatly near the fire circle.

Jonathan and Amanda had been in Scouts. They built a tiny tepee with scraps of dried birchbark and twigs from dead trees. It took only one match. In minutes, a hot fire was burning the larger pieces of wood. Grampa leaned back against Tecumseh, content. When only hot coals remained, Grampa got up and put the foil-wrapped potatoes in the center and the fish and vegetables around the edges. Amanda opened a package of crackers and Jonathan cut up Grampa's favorite cheddar cheese.

The forest was becoming still as shadows lengthened. Quietly munching cheese and crackers, the three musketeers waited for their supper to cook. It was so peaceful. Grampa was silent. He seemed to be enjoying all the changes evening was bringing to the glen. The red-tailed hawk was again circling, but now much lower.

"Of course, you know that the American eagle is a symbol of our country's freedom, but did you know that hawks and eagles were especially sacred to the American Indians?" Grampa asked. The twins shook their heads.

Grampa continued, "Indians believed hawks and eagles were very special. The feathers of the beautiful eagle were revered and used only by chiefs and the bravest warriors to decorate their ceremonial war bonnets and peace pipes."

Grampa paused and closed his eyes. I remember, a long time ago, Grampa Daniel and I watched a circling American eagle right here. It's a sight no one forgets." He opened his eyes and smiled.

There was no eagle tonight, but Jonathan and Amanda were hypnotized by the beauty and grace of the red-tailed hawk, which effortlessly soared above them. "Time to eat," Grampa announced, smiling. And the children came down to earth.

It was a wonderful meal, the first of many Amanda and Jonathan enjoyed with Grampa under Tecumseh's branches. The fish was delicious. Grampa told them of times he and Nana had enjoyed a fish dinner under Tecumseh's branches while watching the sun set. A rare treat was when an elk or two would come to drink from the river. Grampa said the Indians called elk "wapiti."

The children washed the dishes and put the food away as the sun faded behind the mountains. Jonathan placed the fish bones near the river for the raccoons and they all settled under Tecumseh's branches to wait. Grampa was right. Soon a mother and two baby raccoons stopped on their nightly journey to eat the scraps. After the little bandits ate in the fading light, everyone silently watched the mother raccoon teach her youngsters how to catch crayfish. The mother raccoon caught one right away but the young ones groped and splashed here and there without success. After several futile attempts, the young raccoons shook their heads and turned to their mother with the saddest looks. Jonathan and Amanda held their hands over their mouths so they wouldn't laugh out loud. Then one by one, following each other, the raccoons ambled off.

Alone again, the family sat in silence watching embers of the fire slowly die and listening to sounds of the night. Stars twinkled above the mountaintops silhouetted by the final moments of the afterglow. Grampa raised his eyes to the horizon and as if in church, softly recited his favorite poem describing mountains. Then he pointed out several constellations that Indians and sailors used to guide them at night.

"Whoo,whoo,whoo,whoo!" broke the silence.

"That's a great horned owl sending you his greetings," Grampa said with a chuckle.

Jonathan and Amanda had snuggled next to Grampa, who had his arms around them. Amanda wondered what Jonathan was thinking, and wasn't surprised when he asked, "Grampa, why did our dad have to die? Why a car accident? Why him?" Jonathan tried to hold back his tears, but when Amanda began to sob, Jonathan cried too. Grampa held the children tighter before he spoke.

"No one I know," Grampa began, "can give you that answer. Nana and I have asked ourselves the same question thousands of times and wept a million tears. Jeff, as you know, was our only son, and the pain of his death will always be with us. I can think of nothing harder in life than to accept the loss of someone we dearly love! Only tears and time will lessen the anger, bitterness, grief and emptiness we feel. Eventually the intensity of these feelings will be diminished by the wonderful memories we have of your dad   our son. Maybe tomorrow I can show you something in the forest that will make it a little easier for you to accept your father's death. Besides that, I can only tell you what other people believe, and what I believe.

"We know life is a precious gift. Many of the world's great religions say that the soul or spirit of every person lives on after death. I know Indians believed this. They believed that when a person died, their spirit would be carried on the wings of an eagle to a beautiful, safe and happy land—a land with an abundance of food and game. In many ways, Indian beliefs, your father's beliefs and mine are very similar. Native Americans had many wonderful ideas. They believed deeply that humans should share the world with all the plants and creatures made by the Great Spirit. Everyone and every-thing is connected. Father Sky, Mother Earth and the spirits of the sun and rain made it possible for all plants and animals to survive and grow. When the Indians harvested crops or killed game for food they thanked the spirit of the plant or animal for giving up its life so they might live."

"Nana and I have been fortunate to have lived a long and happy life. Every spring, we watch new plants burst through the ground and little baby animals appear with their parents in the forest. Most survive, grow, live a long and happy life, and get old until, as the Indians say, it is time for their bodies to die and their spirits to rest in the spirit world. This day comes for every creature, and when I die I do not want you to be sad for me. Yes, you will miss me as I will miss you, but I believe that in my heaven, there will be trees like Tecumseh, laughing waters, peace and love. Wherever that is, I believe your father is there now and we will see him again.

"Let me tell you a little bit more about your father. Remember when we played gin rummy in the kitchen with Nana, your Mom and Dad? All of us were given cards. Each of us had to play them as best we could. Life is the same way. We can't change where we were born, our parents or grandparents, our size, looks or physical abilities or disabilities. As you know, your father was born without a left hand. Did it stop him from doing many things?"

"No," the twins murmured.

Grampa continued, "My son loved every minute of life. We often talked right here under Tecumseh's branches. Jeff became a pretty good baseball player even with only one hand. A couple of major league ballplayers by the names of Pete Gray and Jim

Abbott were his heroes.

"Later in school, he decided long-distance running might be good for him, and he became one of his college's finest. His hero was a small man with a big heart by the name of Johnny Kelley. Your father began running marathons, which are 26 miles. One of his greatest thrills was running in the Boston Marathon when he was only twenty-two and Johnny Kelley was approaching 80 years old. For a few minutes, they ran side by side.

"After he graduated, Jeff had the opportunity to spend a year in a foreign country. He discovered that he loved learning a new language and being part of another culture. When he returned to college, he combined his interest in languages with engineering. When he graduated, he was able to find a job with an international company. Your father was sent all over the world, building everything from bridges to skyscrapers.

"He met your mom, they fell in love and married. Jeff traveled, less but I know you remember some of things he brought both of you from distant lands."

Amanda spoke first, "I think I have dolls from a dozen different countries." And then she looked at Jonathan.

"Dad brought me so many things," Jonathan added. "I guess the camel saddle from Egypt and the Woodsman Nutcracker from Germany are my favorites. I still sit on that camel saddle when I want to do some heavy thinking."

Grampa nodded and continued, "Your father lived every day to the fullest. He had a wonderful wife and two terrific children—all of whom he loved very much. Jeff often told me how lucky he was. We often spoke about the fact that no one lives forever and what really counts is the quality of each day we live."

The children's tears had stopped. Grampa's words had helped.

The shadows of dusk moved silently toward the still sunlit mountain peaks. It seemed as if an invisible hand was holding a giant flashlight and directing a beam toward the mountain tops as darkness blanketed the rest of the world. Grampa's eyes were on the mountains, too.

Silently above a whisper, Grampa spoke:

"The frail spirit of man has ever searched for—and often found—
strength in the shadows of the mountains—"

"That beautiful piece of poetry was written by Winston O. Abbott, who loved nature and our world. He had a wonderful way with words."

"Grampa," Amanda began, "there is something else that has been bothering us. Remember we told you about Mr. Dubin, mother's friend. Well, we know they like each other a lot and we like him too. He seems to really care about us. We call him Michael, which is fine with him. I don't think we could ever call him Father or Dad. What bothers us is, Mr. Dubin doesn't go to our church. He goes to temple on Friday nights. What will happen if he and Mom get married? Will we have to go to temple too?"

Grampa poked at the fire with a marshmallow stick. "You are really giving me some tough questions tonight," he replied. "Well, let's start with the word 'love.' If Mr. Dubin loves you and your mom as much as I think, the differences in religious backgrounds won't stop you from becoming a happy family. Today you may not be able to picture him as your father, but someday you may. As you grow closer as a family, you will want to learn about his beliefs and traditions and he probably will want to learn more about yours. Later in your lives, you will study the different religions of the world and each of you will decide which spiritual path to follow.

"Listen and respect other people's points of view. Your understanding of people and their ideas is important, and open minds never stop growing. As you know, Nana and I go to a different church than you and your mother. You have been to both—are they that much different?"

"No," the twins replied in unison.

"Mr. Dubin sounds like a caring and sensitive man. If you two want the marriage to work and help in every way you can, then I believe it will be wonderful for all of you. I hope one of these weekends you will invite him to come up with your mom so Nana and I can meet him."

"Sounds like a good idea, Grampa," Jonathan chimed in. "Michael is really a neat guy. We like him a lot." Jonathan added another log to the fire and changed the subject to sports. After discussing the chances of their state's professional baseball team to win the pennant, Grampa pointed out different constellations. They talked about stars for a long time. How close they seemed and how far they really were. How people all over the world had used them to navigate at night and as part of their religious beliefs. Grampa explained about light-years. Even at their age, the twins found it really hard to understand anything being so far away.

"You know, kids," Grampa said half seriously "you might be the first set of astronaut twins to travel to another planet. I can see it now...both of you standing on Mars, waving to me." A big grin spread over his face. "You will wave, won't you?"

"Of course we will!" Amanda said. "In fact, I'll make up a sign for Jonathan to hold that will say *Hi, Grampa, Nana and Tecumseh, too!*" They all laughed. Then Grampa said it was late and future astronauts needed sleep like everyone else. Jonathan and Amanda got their toothpaste and toothbrushes and brushed their teeth in the silvery moonlight at the river's edge. Then they kissed their Grampa good night.

Chapter III

"The first thing Jonathan was aware of the next morning was the smell of wood smoke and bacon sizzling in a frying pan. Grampa's and Amanda's sleeping bags were empty. Jonathan could feel the sun heating up the tent. He stuck his head through the flaps.

"Good afternoon, sleepyhead," Amanda shouted, "would you like some supper?"

"Very funny," Jonathan replied with half a smile, because he was really only half awake. By the time Jonathan got dressed and washed, Grampa had the pancake batter all ready. He handed Jonathan the spatula. "Chef Amanda has cooked the bacon. Will Chef Jonathan do the pancake honors?"

"*Mais oui*," Jonathan replied. But his first attempt at flipping a pancake was a disaster. It went up fine, turned over, but it missed the frying pan and went hissing angrily into the flames.

"We may starve, Grampa, unless Jonathan improves rapidly," Amanda laughed. Grampa gravely nodded, but Jonathan saw the twinkle in his eye and he poured more batter in the frying pan. Jonathan's second attempt succeeded, and from then on it was a "piece of cake."

It was a great breakfast—Grampa told the children about one breakfast he and Nana had prepared at this spot but never got to eat. Nana and Grampa had picked fat, juicy blueberries the night before and were looking forward to blueberry pancakes for breakfast. According to Grampa, the batter was all made, and just as he was about to pour the first pancake he looked up and saw a brown bear ambling along the shore in their direction. He put down the pan and spatula, took Nana's hand, and without a word they quickly headed up the hill looking for a pine tree to climb.

By the time they got to a tree and looked back, the bear had sniffed his way to their campsite. In less than a minute the bear's nose disappeared into the pancake batter pot, and seconds later the bear was licking it clean. With pancake batter dripping from his snout, the bear looked very funny, but only Grampa chuckled. Nana was thinking of all the time she had spent picking those blueberries.

"Blueberry face!" Nana whispered. The bear sniffed a bit more and then peered directly up the hill, nodded as if saying "Thank you," and continued on his way.

"Are there bears around here now?" Amanda asked Grampa.

"No, it's very rare to see a bear nowadays," Grampa answered. "If a bear is seen anywhere nearby, the national park rangers trap it and take it deeper into the park before letting it go, so the chances of seeing one are very small."

After breakfast, Jonathan put water on to make cocoa and also to wash the dishes. By 10 a.m. they had packed up everything and were ready to take the long way back to Grampa's home. At first they followed the river for an hour, weaving in and out of the beautiful white birches. Grampa paused every little while to point out rabbit holes, deer hoofprints, various animal droppings and raccoon dens. Grampa spotted some porcupine quills. He told the twins how Indians used the quills to decorate leggings, headdresses and peace pipe stems. As they walked, Grampa talked about the different trees that grew along the way. He explained why the weeping willow grows only near water and how the gray and white birches provided the bark for the Indians' canoes. Grampa pointed out sugar maples in a meadow that he had tapped years ago for maple syrup. The twins thought, "Grampa was wilderness country's walking, talking encyclopedia." Then they turned toward the forest.

When Grampa spotted a different tree, they stopped and he explained how its leaves or bark were unique. They stopped beside red and white pines to count their needles, which grow in clumps of three or five. The deeper they walked into the forest, the darker and denser it became. Tall pine trees grew side by side with their branches touching. Grampa knew where he was going. Jonathan and Amanda were lost.

"There it is!" Grampa explained, "this way." Following Grampa, the twins pushed the branches aside and ducked under limbs to try to keep up. Grampa had stopped at the edge of a small opening. He stood before a pine that had no needles on any of its branches. Halfway up, the tree was split open, and a black scar led down the trunk into the ground.

"Remember last night we talked about your dad?" Grampa began. The twins nodded and waited for him to continue.

"Well, this dead tree in the middle of the forest was the same size as thousands of other trees that are still standing and growing nearby. Why did lightning hit this particular tree? No one will ever know. It just did."

"Years ago, I read a wonderful book entitled 'When Bad Things Happen to Good People.' Part of the author's answer was that sometimes bad things just happen—period! It is hard to understand, I know, yet we must simply accept that good things and bad things are part of life. Does that make any sense to you two?"

"Yes," the twins whispered.

Grampa smiled. "You will cherish memories of your father as I do, and his spirit will always be with us."

"Now, can you point me in the right direction?" Grampa asked.

Jonathan and Amanda looked at the sun and the shadows of the trees, which were beginning to lengthen. The campsite, they knew, was north of Nana's and Grampa's house, so they pointed in a southerly direction.

"I tell everyone my grandchildren are very bright and you proved it again. Right on the button! If we follow the direction you indicated, we will cross *Nana's Walk* in less than an hour. I'll break the trail, watch the branches—follow me." Grampa began to whistle the work song of the Seven Dwarfs. Amanda and Jonathan joined in.

The twins had a wonderful vacation with Nana and Grampa and went fishing and camping several more times. On each trip they learned more about the woods, its creatures and of the Indians' way of life. Grampa told them about the earliest Indians, who learned to cook by heating stones and putting them in tightly woven baskets that held water—stone boilers. Grampa explained how Indians made birchbark canoes and traps to catch all types of game. The twins learned the names and history of many courageous and wise Native Americans who fought to preserve their way of life and culture. Chiefs like Sitting Bull, Tecumseh, Chief Joseph, Standing Bear, Chief Seattle and many others. They even learned an Indian prayer. Around their grandparents' home, the twins helped Nana and Grampa with their garden. Side by side they planted and weeded. In fact, Jonathan and Amanda had a little patch of their own. They planted some carrots, beets and cucumbers.

The weeks flew by and the children went home two weeks before the beginning of school. On Labor Day weekend, they convinced Mom and Michael to take them to Grampa's to see their garden.

Michael was very interested in everything. At supper, he told the twins their fresh vegetables were the best he had eaten all year.

Michael and Grampa liked each other right off. Grampa showed him around the old homestead and related its history during a short walk in the woods. After supper, Grampa took out some old albums with black and white photos of "kinfolk." Everyone asked Nana and Grampa lots of questions about the people in the pictures. There was even one with Grampa Daniel and a brown bear he had killed because it had taken several of Grampa Daniel's sheep.

Grampa said, "Sheep were mighty important in those days, as Grampa's wife, Jane, would spin the wool and make clothing for the family. Of course, the sheep provided meat too."

By the end of the weekend, the twins, their mother and Michael had seen the original wells that were built for water, old lanterns that had burned whale oil and a few of the old handmade tools Grampa had carefully saved. One night he took out his "very special box." One by one Grampa unwrapped almost one hundred Indian artifacts collected over the years. He had many different shaped and colored Indian arrow points, but none as beautiful as the one he carried. Grampa told where each artifact was found and what he believed each piece was used for: stone fishing weights, round atlatls (spear-throwing weights), chipped ax heads and knives of stone and metal.

Grampa's favorites were stone pipe bowls. He picked up a cherry-colored stone bowl. "This is my best piece!" he exclaimed. "The Indian who made this ceremonial bowl pipe was a gifted craftsman. Indians believe that when the stem is inserted into the bowl, the pipe becomes spiritually alive. This wonderful pipe was used only on very special occasions and was made from rare and sacred Catlinite."

Amanda held the bowl pipe first. "If only this beautiful piece of stone could tell us about its creator," she wondered out loud. Then she passed it to Jonathan.

Nana said, "These are real antiques, but Grampa would never sell them."

"Nana's right," Grampa continued, "They represent life, our link to the past, our own ancestors and the family of man." Michael agreed they were priceless, and said some day we would value them as much as Grampa did.

The twins knew he was right. Just learning about where their ancestors came from, how they lived and the Indians that lived near made them feel different—maybe a little more related to everything and everyone. Later when Amanda and Jonathan talked about Grampa's pictures and artifacts, it seemed that knowing a little of their past made them feel more confident about their own future. They didn't know why—it just did.

Chapter IV

The summer was definitely over. Amanda and Jonathan returned to school. One fall evening at supper, Mom asked the question they had been expecting for some time. She and Michael wanted to get married, and how would the twins feel about it?

Jonathan and Amanda had talked about it for hours. They told their mother they knew Mr. Dubin was a good man and they liked him very much. If she loved him, they would do everything they could to make them a happy family. Their mother broke into tears. The twins didn't mention their talk with Grampa and didn't say much more. They just hugged their mother for a long time.

Two nights later, the twins were on the phone to Nana and Grampa telling them they were invited to a Christmas/Hanukkah wedding. Their grandparents had many questions, and the children turned the phone over to their mother. She explained that she and Michael would be married by a minister and a rabbi at a nice hotel that had a lovely room. The guest list would be about 100 people, and after the wedding there would be a buffet and dancing. Amanda loved that, and Jonathan thought of his two left feet. He knew he would survive, but he wondered if the feet of his partners would too.

Before goodbyes were said, Grampa got on the phone and said to Jonathan, "Practice up your two-step, my boy. There'll be lots of pretty girls there and we don't want them leaving on crutches." Grampa laughed. "Just kidding, son."

Jonathan laughed too and told his Grampa that he planned to wear a sign saying, "dance with me at your own risk." Grampa thought that was pretty funny.

Six weeks later the big day arrived. "Amanda looks beautiful in her new dress," Jonathan thought, "even if she is my sister."

Amanda was thinking, "Jonathan looks really handsome and debonair in his black and white tux—even if he is my brother."

Everything was just perfect. The weather cooperated—it was a beautiful winter day. The ceremony went off without a hitch. The twins' mom and Michael were married. Everyone thought it was a beautiful wedding.

Then came the the food. It was unbelievable! For a growing boy, like Jonathan, it was Christmas and Hanukkah rolled into one. Women members of the two families brought their special dishes for the buffet. The array of food was mind-boggling. From Michael's side of the family there were knishes (little pastries stuffed with potato), chopped liver, brisket of beef, kugel (noodle pudding), and stuffed cabbage, just to name a few.

Nana made her chicken with marmalade sauce, homemade baked beans, and lots of fresh vegetable dishes. Aunts and friends had brought scallop casseroles and shrimp and beef dishes. The overloaded dessert table sagged with apple and pumpkin pies, cheesecake, macaroons, and chocolate goodies as far as the eye could see. You name it—Jonathan ate it. Compliments flowed from one side of the room to the other. "Congratulations," "Mazeltov," "Hello," "Shalom," echoed from wall to wall. Soon, Jewish and gentile recipes were being written down and tucked away like treasures. Nobody could say enough about the food, except maybe Jonathan. He just kept eating.

The band played music, old and new, so everyone was happy. Amanda and Jonathan danced first with Mom and Michael, then Nana and Grampa, and later with Michael's nieces and nephews. They learned some Jewish line dances, and even Nana and Grampa got on the dance floor with Michael's grandparents. The twins liked Michael's mother and father and his friends too. By the end of the afternoon it seemed as if it was simply one big joyous family.

Amanda and Jonathan talked with Nana and Grampa a lot. Grampa seemed a bit tired and a little thinner than when they had seen him on their last visit. He and Nana said they were having a wonderful time and were looking forward to staying with the twins over Christmas while Mom and Michael went on their honeymoon.

The following week, Jonathan and Amanda still had two days of school, so they got up early. Nana was always an hour ahead of them to make sure they had a good breakfast. They didn't see Grampa until they got home. As usual, he was happy to see them and wanted to know all about their day. By the end of supper, Grampa needed to rest. Sometimes when the twins came downstairs after doing their homework to kiss Nana and Grampa good night, Grampa was fast asleep in the big stuffed chair.

Mom and Michael returned home. They showed everyone postcards, pictures, and souvenirs from their trip. They had bought beautiful handmade, matching sweaters for Nana and Grampa.

Jonathan and Amanda received lovely sweaters too. That night, they celebrated their Christmas/Hanukkah dinner and opened gifts from one another. It was indeed a wonderful evening.

The next day after breakfast, Nana and Grampa got ready to return to their home. After lots of hugs and kisses, Nana helped Grampa with his topcoat and he held her jacket.

"Next time you visit Tecumseh, give him our best, Grampa," Jonathan called, as Grampa and Nana slowly walked down the front steps.

At the bottom of the steps, Grampa turned, and for a moment the old smile and twinkle returned to his eyes. "You can bet on that kids—study hard and call us soon!" Grampa, slightly bent over, slowly shuffled to the passenger side of the car. Nana was going to drive. The twins looked at each other. Grampa always drove.

Even though it was vacation, the twins had school projects to do, so they headed up the stairs to their rooms. They stopped at the top step. There was a plain white box with a blue ribbon. A tag was tied on top. In Grampa's handwriting it said, TO AMANDA AND JONATHAN. Jonathan picked it up.

"Go ahead, you open it, Amanda." It only took a moment. Inside, wrapped in white tissue paper, was Grampa's favorite Indian artifact, the cherry-colored stone pipe bowl and Nana's beautiful atlatl. The twins remembered Grampa had told them it was an Indian tradition to leave gifts where friends and family would find them. These gifts meant a lot to both Amanda and Jonathan, but they wondered why Grampa and Nana had given them these gifts now. They agreed to find a special place for them and went to their rooms to write Grampa and Nana thank-you notes.

It was a busy, busy year for the children. Afternoon basketball practices, nightly homework and daily chores left little extra time. However, at least once a week they called their grandparents. Most of the time, Nana would answer and Grampa would come to the phone and talk for a few minutes. His voice seemed weak and tired, but he always asked about the twins' games and classes. Nana sounded fine. Amanda and Jonathan were concerned about Grampa. Finally, they asked Nana if Grampa was all right. Nana told them that Grampa was seeing a doctor and not to worry. But they did worry.

Early in May, Nana called. Mom said Nana wanted the family to come and see Grampa on the weekend.

Jonathan rang the doorbell. The family waited anxiously. Seconds later, Nana opened the door. She smiled broadly and hugged and kissed everyone before leading them to the living room. Nana looked tired. Amanda and Jonathan sat next to her on the couch and she put her arms around them.

"Where's Grampa?" Jonathan asked in a shaky voice.

Nana took a deep breath, showed a hint of a smile and began. "You know Grampa is ill. We made the downstairs den into a bedroom for him. You can go see him in just a few moments, but first I want to talk with you. During the last few months Grampa has been very sick. He has lost a lot of weight and doesn't look much like the big, strong man you have known and remember. Grampa likes to sit in a wheelchair during the day next to the window. He naps a lot. A visiting nurse from Hospice comes in the morning and at night to help me wash Grampa and get him in and out of bed. When he is awake, Grampa is still very sharp and the twinkle is still in his eye.

"The doctors at the hospital have told us they have done all they can. Grampa and I decided the best place for him was home."

Jonathan and Amanda were not surprised to hear the news and thought of all the things Grampa had said about life and death, but that couldn't stop their tears.

Nana spoke again. "Now dry your eyes, all of you. Replace those terribly sad faces with smiles. Grampa and I are tired but not sad. We have had a wonderful life together and believe we will be together again."

Finally Mom, Amanda and Jonathan got their sobbing under control and they followed Nana down the hall to Grampa's room.

"Hi, Grampa!" the twins chorused, and ran to kiss him. He was so thin it was tough not to cry. Mom and Michael came in and hugged and kissed Grampa.

The loving smile and twinkling eyes looked up, "How are my grown-up twins doing? Jonathan, have you married Ashley yet?"

"Not yet, Grampa. I'm waiting to see if she is going to graduate from junior high, high school and college."

Grampa laughed weakly. "Good answer and good thinking, son. Amanda, are you still breaking hearts and being number one in your class?"

Amanda smiled, "Well, not many hearts, and Jonathan is a very close second academically."

As Amanda and Jonathan talked, they each held one of Grampa's hands. Mom and Michael went to help Nana in the kitchen. Grampa listened as the twins described all that was happening at school and the teams they played on. As they talked, Grampa seemed agitated, as if he wanted to ask a question, yet was afraid of the answer he might receive. The twins knew Grampa well.

Jonathan asked him point blank, "Grampa, tell us, what do you want?" For a moment, his head dropped. The twins thought he wanted to take a nap. Grampa squeezed their hands, raised his head and looked directly at them.

"Please," he began, "take me to see Tecumseh one more time." His gaze didn't move as he waited for their answer.

For a moment, Amanda and Jonathan didn't know what to say. They knew how important Tecumseh's Glen was to Grampa.

Without thinking they said, "Yes, Grampa, we will." Grampa smiled, closed his eyes and instantly fell asleep.

Mom, Michael and Nana were talking at the kitchen table. The cookie jar was almost full and Mom brought the twins some milk but they weren't hungry. Michael spoke first, "Have some cookies—you know how much Grampa and Nana enjoy watching you empty the cookie jar."

"Please," Nana echoed.

"Thank you, Nana." the twins replied, and they each took a cookie. Jonathan and Amanda looked at each other. Jonathan nodded and Amanda said, "We made Grampa a promise."

"We promised to take Grampa to Tecumseh's Glen tomorrow," Jonathan continued. "We couldn't say no. We promised."

None of the adults spoke for a long time. "I understand," their mom began quietly, "but is it possible or wise? Grampa is very sick and weak." Then she looked at Michael and Nana.

Michael spoke first. "It might be possible, since it hasn't rained in a few weeks. For May, the earth is unusually dry and the ground is hard. The wheelchair could be pushed and pulled fairly easily. The little hill before Tecumseh's Glen will be difficult, but if the weather holds for twenty-four hours, it could be done. The forecast, though, is not good. Is it a wise thing to do? Only Nana should answer that part of your mother's question."

They all looked at Nana and waited for her to speak. Her eyes seemed brighter and a sad-happy look covered her face.

"I'm not surprised at Grampa's request," she said." What was the expression I heard recently on TV?" She thought a moment, then smiled. "Oh yes," she said, "your Grampa is a piece of work."

For the first time since they entered Nana and Grampa's home, everyone laughed. Nana continued, "You know how much Grampa loves Tecumseh's Glen—we both do. In fact, our ashes will be taken there. If my grandchildren and Michael think it is possible, then Grampa should have his wish. Nothing we can do will make him better, but if see-

ing and touching Tecumseh one more time is what he wants, then we can make him happy. We will all go. Grampa would want it to be a picnic. Jonathan and Amanda, get the backpacks out. You and Michael can find everything we might need. Gail and I will make the sandwiches and fill the thermoses."

First Michael, Jonathan and Amanda made a list of everything they might need. In less than an hour the backpacks were ready. Mom and Nana said the food was made and wrapped. All agreed they should leave soon after dawn. Moments later, the visiting nurse arrived. She and Nana got Grampa ready for sleep, and the nurse promised to return very early. Then everyone said good night and the family went straight to bed.

At sunrise, Grampa was dressed for the journey. He seemed to be stronger. He smiled a lot. His eyes were brighter and he tried to help as much as he could. Finally, the family had him dressed warmly and bundled tightly in the wheelchair.

"Ready, Grampa?" Jonathan asked.

Nana had told the twins that whenever Grampa faced a new challenge a look of fierce determination and at the same time happiness would spread across his face—the look was there. Stronger than yesterday, Grampa spoke, "I'm ready!"

Outdoors, ropes were tied to both arm rests in case they were needed. Jonathan began pushing. It was fairly easy as the group entered the forest and followed *Nana's Walk*. Michael and Amanda walked in front, loosely holding the ropes. Nana and Mom walked behind. Grampa was wide awake and his head moved slowly side to side as if he were trying to photograph everything he saw.

The sun was fully awake too. Its bright rays filtered through the pines. It was a beautiful day. Amanda, Michael and Jonathan took turns pushing Grampa. Here and there, early spring wildflowers had blossomed. The smell of the pines and the new life of spring was wonderful. Everyone smiled as Grampa hummed his favorite songs. In less than two hours they came to the hill before Tecumseh's Glen. Michael and Jonathan took the ropes and pulled while Amanda guided and steadied the wheelchair. With a little huffing and puffing, all were soon atop the hill and paused to enjoy the view. The glen was a magnificent spring green and, as always, Tecumseh stood straight and tall. The beautiful Manitou River appeared to be a shimmering silver road. A gentle breeze carried the voices of its laughing stones.

Carefully, the trio guided Grampa down the hill until they stopped beside Tecumseh. Grampa slowly reached out until he touched the rough old bark of his friend. He turned back and looked up smiling. In a strong whisper he said, "Thank you all."

Nana and Mom quickly spread a blanket on the ground near Tecumseh and unloaded the food pack. It didn't take long before the sandwiches began to disappear. Everyone had worked up an appetite from the morning's trek. Even Nana was able to get Grampa to drink some water and take several small bites from a sandwich. Grampa seemed very content.

The warm sun and food made everyone sleepy. Jonathan and Michael, having finished eating, were lying back basking in the sun. Nana and Mom were storing the left-overs, and Grampa remained sitting next to Tecumseh, one hand resting on his friend. Just as his granddaughter decided to lie back and rest too, Grampa whispered, "Amanda."

Amanda looked at Grampa, who was pointing one finger at the sky behind him. She followed his finger and saw that a front of rolling gray thunder clouds was moving fast in their direction. "Michael, Jonathan," she called, "look!"

The air had become cooler and the wind direction had changed. "We better get moving fast," Jonathan said. "If I am right, those storm clouds contain lots of rain, and if the hill becomes a sea of mud we'll never make it to the top. Let's go."

Everything was packed quickly and the straps that held Grampa in the wheelchair were checked. Everyone put on rain ponchos and Grampa was wrapped up tight.

Grampa seemed to welcome the race against the weather and time. He knew it was late. It was going to be a rocky ride home. Having spent much of his life outdoors in the fiercest weather, Grampa respected the power of nature, yet he believed that the man or woman who prepared for the worst would survive. Michael, Jonathan and Amanda knew their planning was about to be tested. Just as they moved slowly up the hill it began to sprinkle.

Michael and Jonathan, harnessed like two horses, pulled the wheelchair foot by foot up the hill. At first the rain was light. Jonathan and Michael only fell once. Fortunately, Amanda had secure footing and was able to hold Grampa's wheelchair from slipping backward. As the men neared the top, the real rain began. Michael and Jonathan had to crawl to avoid falling. Progress was very, very slow. Finally they reached the brow of the hill.

Jonathan stood up and smiled. Rain-streaked mud covered his face. He really looked funny, but nobody laughed. "Well," he said, "the tough work of the hill is done—now the tricky work begins." Michael and Amanda listened to Jonathan's plan as Nana and Mom continued slowly on, one helping the other. Michael suggested that Gail and Nana get home as quickly as possible to prepare for Grampa's arrival. Jonathan shifted the ropes to the back of the wheelchair and brought out more rope to lengthen each run. He took one rope and looped it around a pine tree to the right and then took the other rope and ran it around another pine on the left.

The men eased the wheelchair down while Amanda tried to keep Grampa from turning over. Holding tightly to the handlebars of the wheelchair, Grampa began the descent. Amanda dug her heels into the mud and looked for secure footing so she wouldn't slip and crash into Grampa.

As the wind whipped the hood of Grampa's parka back and forth, Amanda would occasionally get a glimpse of his head and face. His thin hair was matted flat from the rain that poured down over eyes, cheeks and chin. Yet he looked full of life, unafraid, determined—even happy. He seemed to be thinking, "Weather, do your worst. I've a smart, tough, crew with me and they won't let you beat them." Amanda read Grampa's mind and hoped he was right.

It seemed like years before they were on the flat. Michael and Jonathan again tied the ropes across their chests and began to pull. But now, even in the woods, the soggy ground made going very slow. The wheelchair's wheels, clogged with mud, no longer turned, making the wheelchair very difficult to pull. The wind tore at the parkas and the rain came down in sheets. Hours passed, and finally the drenched band reached the little brook that usually one could step across—but not now. A wide and growing, raging stream lay before them.

Mom and Nana were nowhere to be seen. They must have crossed the brook before it became a torrent. Jonathan, Amanda and Michael discussed the situation. Amanda volunteered to cross first to see how deep the water was at this spot and determine the footing below the rushing waters. A rope was tied around her waist. Gingerly, Amanda stepped into water, feeling for a hard bottom. The water swirled above her knees. By sliding her feet cautiously along the bottom, she crossed safely in a few minutes.

Jonathan and Michael then entered the water. Holding Grampa out of the water, they moved slowly, feeling their way. Just as they reached the middle of the stream, Jonathan caught his foot on an underwater branch and lost his balance and began to fall. "Let go of the wheelchair," Michael shouted. Jonathan did, and disappeared below the water. A second later he popped up near the shore, sputtering. Michael was straining every muscle. He was holding Grampa above the water by himself as Jonathan desperately fought the stream to get back. Only a minute passed, but it seemed forever before Jonathan was again holding his side of the wheelchair. Michael smiled, "Onward and upward," he shouted, and they again moved in unison toward the bank.

Amanda put out her hand and guided the wheelchair to solid ground. Michael and Jonathan flopped down beside Grampa, who was now definitely very tired. He had had enough excitement. Everyone was soaked through and through. Amanda dug into her backpack and found three big chocolate bars. It took less than a minute for the three to eat them. Jonathan and Michael staggered to their feet. It was late in the afternoon and becoming dark. Jonathan gave his flashlight to Amanda as he and Michael harnessed up once more. With luck, in another hour they would be home. The rain continued to come down in torrents.

It was close to two hours before they reached Grampa's back porch. Nana, Mom and the nurse rushed outside and took Grampa inside. Michael, Amanda and Jonathan sat on the back porch for a few minutes, trying to find a little more energy to drag themselves inside.

Michael had given his all. His arms were wrapped around the twins. Amanda was resting her head against his shoulder and Jonathan sat on his other side. Jonathan looked up with a tired but satisfied smile, reached out and shook Michael's hand and said, "Thanks, Dad." Amanda, opened her eyes, gave Michael a kiss on his muddy cheek and she too said, "Thanks, Dad." Michael held back a tear.

Jonathan grinned and thought, "Grampa was right again."

After everyone showered and put on bathrobes, Jonathan and Amanda went in to say good night to Grampa. His eyes were closed, but as they bent down to kiss him he winked and smiled before peacefully falling asleep.

When the twins returned to their home, Amanda and Jonathan sometimes cried when they thought of Grampa. They reminded each other of what he had told them and knew that the quality of life he wanted was gone forever. Grampa was ready for a new experience and was looking forward to meeting his ancestors face to face. He had often told them with a grin, "There will be lots of stories to share."

Nana called often, and sometimes Grampa said a word or two. Almost two months later, the telephone call that the family knew was coming arrived. Grampa had died peacefully during the day.

Nana said that since the twins were their favorite grandchildren (Nana chuckled like Grampa always did when he said that, as the twins were their only grandchildren), Nana wanted them to be part of the memorial service for Grampa, which would be in the fall. Of course, Amanda and Jonathan said yes.

Amanda and Jonathan thought a lot about what they would say.

When the day arrived, the air was crisp, the sun shone through the autumn leaves and the church was full.

First the minister led a prayer. He described how he first met Grampa and the many things Grampa had done for people and for the town. Then he introduced the twins, and they approached the microphone.

The twins had grown a lot during the past year. Jonathan spoke first. He smiled and began, "Everyone in our family and Grampa's friends have shed tears because he has died. Today, when Amanda and I remember what he taught us, we can only smile and feel so very lucky we had such a wonderful Grampa. Edwin was his name, but to Amanda and me he was and always will be simply Grampa. Grampa had a great sense of humor and chose his serious words carefully. He loved life passionately—he loved all living things—even black ants. Grampa believed everyone's life is precious—no one's life is more precious than another. Grampa told us how lucky he was to have married Nana, had a fine son and a wonderful daughter-in-law, and said his grandchildren were special—most days."

The congregation laughed.

"Our minister has related some of the things Grampa did to help people," Jonathan continued. "We never heard those stories. Grampa simply believed that it is everyone's responsibility to make this world in someway a little bit better place to live.

"Amanda and I hope we can follow Grampa's path. He was our friend and guide. We love him very much and know he will always be with us." Jonathan stepped aside and Amanda moved in front of the microphone.

Chapter VI

Amanda went to bed first. By the time her head hit the pillow, she was asleep. Jonathan slept well too, until a dream woke him up. He wasn't sure he believed the dream but he knew he couldn't ignore it. Through the window, Jonathan could see the first rays of the sun beginning to turn black into gray. The only time he could remember waking this early was when they went camping with Grampa. Jonathan dressed and slowly opened his door and tiptoed toward the bathroom. Before he got there, the bathroom door swung open and Amanda, dressed for hiking, stepped out. They were both surprised.

"A dream?" she asked.

Jonathan nodded. "Meet you in the kitchen." Amanda smiled.

The twins didn't speak in the kitchen but had a glass of milk and a muffin. Amanda wrote a note for Nana, Mom and Dad: "Gone to Tecumseh's Glen."

It was a beautiful fall morning. The air was fresh, clean and crisp. Neither one spoke as they followed *Nana's Walk,* wrapped in separate but similar thoughts. Were they crazy believing in a dream? Had their dreams been the same?

By the time they stood atop the ridge looking down on Tecumseh's Glen and the Manitou River, the sun indicated it was about 8 o'clock. The glen was as lovely now as it was the morning they had brought Grampa to see Tecumseh for the last time. Interlaced with the evergreens, the deciduous trees were dressed in their autumn colors, and majestic Tecumseh now wore a mantle of reddish hue.

Jonathan and Amanda stood silently for a moment, but they both knew their journey was not over. Without speaking, the twins descended the hill and walked directly to Tecumseh and touched his bark. They looked at each other, went to the water's edge and separated. Jonathan headed up river and Amanda went downstream. Amanda knew what she was looking for and found it in less than ten minutes. Just as in the dream, there was the fallen white birch tree half in and half out of the river. Near one of its branches, a large rock glittered with quartz. Amanda knelt down and turned it over.

Jonathan was upstream. Moving slowly, he carefully studied the shore between the river and the bank. He was looking for fresh deer tracks. As he walked, Jonathan felt a little foolish, but he followed his dream. Finally he saw the fresh hoof marks and beside them a large, almost pure white stone.

Sitting under Tecumseh's branches deep in thought, Amanda waited for Jonathan. She didn't even hear him approach until he was just a few yards away. Then she stood, smiled and held out her closed fist. Jonathan grinned and did the same. Slowly they opened their hands. In each was a brilliant, perfectly made white arrow point.

It may sound silly, but they both gave Tecumseh a big hug. Amanda looked up at the beautiful old oak tree, smiled and said, "Thank you, Tecumseh."

As Jonathan looked upward, at first he couldn't believe his eyes. "Amanda, look!" he shouted. Soaring above them was a magnificent bird with long brown wings, white tail feathers and a white head. The twins knew it was a rare American bald eagle.

"Thank you too, Grampa," Jonathan whispered. The eagle circled twice and flew off toward the mountains. It was time to go. The twins knew they would return many times during their lifetime to visit Tecumseh. Someday, it would be with their own families. At the ridgeline, they turned once more for a last look at the glen. Between the river and Tecumseh, a large elk and her very young calf stood looking up at them. They could only smile.

There was no longer any pain in their hearts. They knew everything was as it was meant to be. Just as Grampa had said.

A feeling of happiness and well-being filled them. They were at peace. They didn't talk, but silently repeated an Indian prayer Grampa had taught them as they followed *Nana's Walk* home . . .

Walk tall as the trees,
Live strong as the mountains,
Be gentle as the spring winds,
Keep the warmth of the summer sun in your heart,
And the Great Spirit will always be with you.

. . . and all the Nanas, Grampas and Tecumseh smiled.

⇌ *The End* ⇌